The Final Cut

For the Millstein gang —

Enjoy

[signature]

Other books by Fred Bowen
T.J.'s Secret Pitch
The Golden Glove
The Kid Coach
Playoff Dreams
Full Court Fever
Off the Rim

CP
JR

A Peachtree Junior Publication
Published by
Peachtree Publishers, Ltd.
494 Armour Circle NE
Atlanta, Georgia 30324

www.peachtree-online.com

Text © 1999 by Fred Bowen
Illustration © 1999 by Ann G. Barrow

Photo of Michael Jordan reprinted with permission of Dan Sears, *Wilmington Morning Star.*

Photo of Bill Russell reprinted with permission of The National Basketball Hall of Fame.

University of North Carolina Tar Heels trademark and copyright used with permission from the University of North Carolina—Chapel Hill.

Jacket illustration by Ann G. Barrow
Book design by Loraine M. Balcsik
Composition by Melanie M. McMahon

Manufactured in the United States of America
10 9 8 7 6 5 4 3 2 1
First Edition

Library of Congress Cataloging-in-Publication Data
Bowen, Fred.
    The final cut / by Fred Bowen ; illustrated by Ann Barrow. — 1st ed.
        p. cm. — (AllStar sportstory)
        Summary: After tryouts for the school basketball team, eighth graders Zeke,
Eli, Ryan, and Miles find their friendship tested when two of them make the team
and two of them do not.
        ISBN 1-56145-192-4
        [1. Basketball—Fiction.] I. Barrow, Ann, ill. II. Title. III. Series: Bowen, Fred.
Allstar sportstory.
PZ7.B6724Fi 1999
[Fic]—dc21   98-37337
                                                                              CIP
                                                                              AC

The Final Cut

by Fred Bowen

Illustrated by
Ann Barrow

PEACHTREE
ATLANTA

For Peggy, Liam, and Kerry.
My team.

ONE

Ryan Phillips looked around the small huddle of boys standing on the windswept field. It was late afternoon on a crisp autumn day. "First down," he said. "What should we do?"

Eli Powell, the biggest kid in the group, shrugged his shoulders and didn't say anything. Miles DuBow shook his head and said, "I don't know. I just don't want to be the hiker again."

Edward "Zeke" Zilkowski stepped into the middle of the huddle and took charge. "Okay," he said. He used his finger to trace a football pattern on the front of Ryan's sweatshirt. "Ryan, you're going to go down about five steps, fake out to the sidelines, and go long." Ryan studied Zeke's finger as it moved up his sweatshirt and nodded. He glanced over his shoulder. The four boys on the other team were waiting impatiently on the other side of the football. Ryan turned his attention back to the huddle.

Zeke looked up at Eli. "Eli, you go down about seven steps and cut across the middle—" he started.

"What about me?" Miles interrupted, punching Zeke on the shoulder.

"Miles, you hike and stay in to block."

"Again?" Miles protested. "I've hiked way more than Ryan and Eli put together."

"Come on, you're our best hiker," Ryan pleaded.

"There's nothing to hiking," Miles complained.

"That's why you're so good at it," Zeke said, patting Miles on the back.

"I don't see why we're even playing football," Miles muttered. "We should be practicing basketball."

"We've got plenty of time to play hoop," Ryan said. "Come on. Let's play football."

The four boys lined up. Ryan looked across the scrimmage line and eyed his opponent, Dustin Henry. Zeke meanwhile kept his eyes on Dustin's teammate Nathan Harmata.

"Remember, you can't rush in before you count 'three Mississippi,'" Zeke called to

Nathan, who was clearly ready to pounce on Zeke.

"Just hike the ball," Nathan replied, locking eyes with Zeke.

Zeke barked out the signals: "Ready, set, hut one...hut two...hut three."

Ryan broke into a run, and Nathan started counting. "One Mississippi...two...."

On his fifth step, Ryan broke to his right, glanced back at Zeke, and then suddenly changed directions and started sprinting upfield.

"Three Mississippi!" Nathan yelled.

Zeke lofted a long pass toward Ryan, sending the football sailing into the clear October sky. Ryan dashed after it. As the ball started to fall ahead of him, he took a flying leap and stretched out his arms as far as he could. He felt the ball brush against his fingertips, then his body slammed against the dirt. When he looked up, the ball was bouncing awkwardly away. "Incomplete!" Dustin shouted.

Ryan clutched his aching side as he got to his feet.

"Good try," Dustin said as he helped Ryan up. "You had me beat."

Ryan trotted slowly back to the huddle.

"Sorry," Zeke said. "I threw that one a little too long."

"I should have had it," Ryan said, still holding his side.

"You'd better hike it this time," Zeke said to Ryan. Then he turned to Eli and Miles. "Eli, you go down and do a buttonhook. I'll throw it high. Miles, you go down and out."

"Finally," Miles said.

This time Zeke whistled a hard pass right to Eli, who grabbed the ball but was tagged before he could move an inch.

"Good catch, big guy," Ryan said, clapping his hands.

"Third down!" Dustin called. "You guys have two more downs left."

"Tie game, right?" Zeke asked as the teams moved up the field. "Next touchdown wins."

"Yeah," the boys on the other team replied as Ryan and his friends huddled again.

"I can beat Dustin on a long pass," Ryan whispered to Zeke.

"Okay," Zeke said. "You run a long slant from the right side." Then, pointing to Eli, Zeke said, "Eli, you cut across the middle from the left side in case Ryan doesn't get open."

4

Eli nodded.

"I guess I'm hiking again," Miles said, sounding annoyed.

"You're the best, Miles." Zeke smiled. "What can I say?"

Ryan lined up on the right side. He kept his feet straight and stared directly at Dustin. He was careful not to let his face or his position give Dustin any clues about the pattern.

"Ready, set, hut one...hut two...."

Miles hiked the ball back straight and true.

"One Mississippi...two Mississippi....

Ryan ran straight for Dustin, who quickly braced himself for a collision. But at the last instant, Ryan angled to the middle of the field without breaking stride.

"Three Mississippi!"

Zeke let go a long pass, and Ryan took off after the speeding football. His legs were churning and his heart was pumping. He got to the ball in time, reached up, and grabbed it, but it popped out of his hands and tumbled end over end in the air. Ryan didn't miss a step. He stayed with it and the ball fell, spinning, right into his cradled arms. He raced into the end zone and raised the football high in triumph.

Zeke, Eli, and Miles raced down the field, celebrating and shouting as they ran.

"Touchdown!"

"Great catch, Ryan!"

"Great throw, Zeke."

Smiling, Zeke turned to the other team. "You want to play another game?" he asked.

"No," Dustin answered, shaking his head. "We've gotta get going."

The other team left and soon it was just the four friends in the middle of the big field, their shadows growing longer as the sun set.

"You want to play a game with just the four of us?" Zeke asked, twirling the football into the air.

"I'm tired," Miles said, shaking his head. "And anyway, I have to practice my sax." He walked over to the side of the field and picked up his saxophone case.

"We've played enough football," Ryan said. "Miles was right. We've really got to start concentrating on basketball. Intramurals start in a couple of days, and tryouts for the school basketball team are in a month and a half."

"Intramurals! That's just a big word for flunky teams," Zeke said. "You don't even have to try out for intramurals. The gym teachers just put you on a team and you play against other kids in the school. All I care about is making the real school team—the Sligo Stallions. I want to play against the best kids from other schools."

"That's what I'm saying," Ryan argued. "If we want to make the Stallions, we should start practicing now, and plan on playing intramurals. That would give us a head start."

"Come on," Zeke pleaded, looking up at the cloudless sky. "It's football weather."

"I got it," Ryan decided. "Let's go to my house and hang out in the basement. We can play Ping-Pong and Miles can practice his sax."

"Let's play football while we've still got a little light left in the day," Zeke said.

Eli eyed Zeke. "I bet I can beat you at Ping-Pong," he said.

"You're on," Zeke said.

TWO

Ryan walked carefully down the wooden steps and felt along the wall for the light switch.

He flicked the switch and a row of track lights suddenly brightened the large, carpeted basement room. A Ping-Pong table stood in the center of the room and a sagging sofa and a couple of battered easy chairs were pushed against the walls, which were plastered with pennants and posters. Off to the left hung a dartboard. Tucked in the far corner was a small, neat desk with a computer.

As they had a thousand times before, the four boys quickly made themselves at home. Zeke and Eli grabbed the two Ping-Pong paddles off the table.

"Come on, big man," Zeke said, motioning with his paddle to the table. "Let's see who the champ is at this game."

"Hey, wait a minute," Ryan protested. "I'm the champ. I beat both of you guys the last time we played."

"All right, all right," Zeke said, waving Ryan off. "I'll beat you after I beat Eli."

Ryan stepped back and watched the ball flash back and forth across the net. Miles took his saxophone out of its case and started practicing his scales.

"Are you just going to play the same notes over and over again?" Zeke demanded. "Why don't you play a song or something?"

"You can't play a song unless you practice your scales," Miles answered in a know-it-all voice.

"Hey," Ryan said, "doesn't intramural basketball start tomorrow?"

"Nah, it starts in two days," Zeke answered. "They're just going to post the team rosters outside the gym tomorrow."

Eli smashed a forehand that just grazed the corner on Zeke's side of the table.

"You are so lucky," Zeke cried, taking a few practice swings with his paddle. "It's 6–4, your lead."

"You guys signed up for intramurals, didn't you?" Ryan asked.

"Yeah," everyone answered together.

"I hate intramurals, but let's face it, you've got to play intramurals if you want to make the Sligo team," Zeke said. "Coach DeCamp watches all the games."

"When are tryouts for the Sligo team?" Miles asked, taking a break from his practice.

"In about six weeks," Zeke answered as he bounced the ball on the table. "After Thanksgiving and after the intramural games end."

"Come on, quit talking and start playing," Eli complained.

"Do you think we'll all make it?" Ryan asked nervously.

"Sure," Zeke said confidently. "We'll make it, no sweat."

Zeke reached across the table to bend a backhand winner past a shocked Eli. "It's 13–12. My lead, big guy." Zeke smiled. Eli retrieved the ball and tossed it to Zeke.

"But we didn't make the team last year," Ryan noted.

"So what?" Zeke said. "We were just seventh graders last year. Hardly any seventh graders made it. We're eighth graders now."

Zeke pointed his paddle across the table and said, "Look at Eli. He must have grown six inches since last year. And you and Miles are taller too."

"Yeah, Zeke," Eli teased, "you're the only guy who hasn't gotten taller."

"Don't worry," Zeke said. "I'll make the team." He wasn't smiling.

"So we're a little taller. So is everyone else. How do you figure the four of us are going to make it?" Ryan asked.

"Easy. The team is only for seventh and eighth graders," Zeke explained. "There are twelve kids on the team. Last year's team had eight eighth graders and they've graduated. I figure Coach DeCamp will want mostly eighth graders like us."

"Yeah, but the Coach will want some seventh graders on the team, too," Miles pointed out and returned to playing his saxophone.

"Yeah, like the Kaess twins, Alex and Andrew," Ryan said. "They're in the seventh grade and they're really good."

"So what?" Zeke said, unimpressed. "That still leaves five or six spots open."

"Come on, Zeke," Eli said, leaning over the table. "Stop yakking and start serving. It's 15–15. Tie game."

"And what about Johnny Fleming and Frankie Reilly?" Ryan asked. "They didn't make the team last year and they're pretty good."

Eli smacked a quick backhand that skidded past Zeke.

"Hey, will you guys quit talking?" Zeke shouted. "It's making it hard to beat Eli."

Ryan got up, walked over to the desk, and turned on the computer.

"What are you doing?" Zeke asked.

"I'm going to figure out our chances of making the basketball team," Ryan replied.

Zeke and Eli continued their Ping-Pong battle as Miles played an upbeat tune and Ryan sat clicking away on the computer keys.

"Who's that new kid at school?" Ryan asked without looking away from the computer screen. "Is he any good?"

"You mean Matthew Finn?" Eli asked. "Yeah, he's supposed to be real good." Eli looked steadily across the table at Zeke. "It's 20–19, Zeke. My lead. Game point."

Zeke stood bent forward at the waist, twirling his paddle. "Chill out, you guys. I've got to concentrate."

Eli spun a serve across the table and Zeke flipped back a return. The ball whizzed back and forth.

"Don't forget Ian Will," Miles reminded Ryan. "All the Wills can play. Hannah's on the girls' team and their older brother Nathan is really good."

Eli sliced a backhand that just nicked the corner of the table. He smiled a wicked smile at Zeke and threw his hands high in triumph. "All right! I finally beat Zeke!"

Zeke stared at Eli. "I can't believe how lucky you are!" he shouted. Turning to the others, he said, "I would have won if these guys had stopped blabbing."

"What?" Eli exclaimed. "Like I couldn't hear everybody talking? Give me a break. Come on, Ryan. Let's play for the championship."

"Wait a second," Ryan said as he pulled a sheet of paper out of the printer tray. "I want to show you something."

The boys gathered around as Ryan laid the paper on the Ping-Pong table.

"What's so important?" Zeke asked, sending his paddle clattering across the table.

13

*The boys gathered around as Ryan laid
the paper on the Ping-Pong table.*

"It's a list of all the kids I figure have a chance to make the basketball team," Ryan explained.

Just then, Ryan's stepfather poked his head into the basement room. "Hi. How are you guys doing?"

"Hi, Max. Just playing some Ping-Pong."

"Well, you guys had better get going. It's almost dinnertime. Ryan, you need to set the table. Your mom and Natalie will be home soon. I'm making chicken enchiladas."

"Okay. I'll be up in a minute."

When Max headed back upstairs, the boys looked at the list of names.

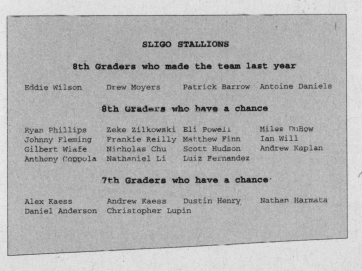

```
              SLIGO STALLIONS

        8th Graders who made the team last year

Eddie Wilson      Drew Moyers    Patrick Barrow  Antoine Daniels

           8th Graders who have a chance

Ryan Phillips    Zeke Zilkowski  Eli Powell     Miles DuBow
Johnny Fleming   Frankie Reilly  Matthew Finn   Ian Will
Gilbert Wiafe    Nicholas Chu    Scott Hudson   Andrew Kaplan
Anthony Coppola  Nathaniel Li    Luiz Fernandez

           7th Graders who have a chance

Alex Kaess       Andrew Kaess    Dustin Henry   Nathan Harmata
Daniel Anderson  Christopher Lupin
```

"Sure are a lot of names there," Miles said uncomfortably.

"Don't worry, we'll make it," Zeke said. "And in two months we'll all be teammates."

THREE

The noises of a new week surrounded Ryan as he hurried down the school corridor. The excited talk and laughter of the students mixed with the metal clanging of slamming lockers. Ryan glanced at his watch.

I only have five minutes to get down to the gym and check out the intramural basketball rosters before World Studies, he thought as he quickly weaved his way through the crowded hallway.

"Hey, Ryan!"

Ryan slowed down and look over his shoulder. Jessica Abell, a classmate and a player on last year's girls' basketball team, was hurrying to catch up with him.

"Are you heading to the gym?" she asked.

"Yeah." Ryan nodded.

"Me, too." Jessica smiled and the two started off again in matching strides.

"Are you playing intramurals?" Ryan asked.

"Sure, Coach Franklin wants all the best girl players to play intramurals," Jessica said. "You've gotta play if you want to make the Sligo team."

"You'll make the team, again, easy," Ryan said, "won't you?"

"I don't know. I guess."

Ryan and Jessica turned the corner that led to the gym. At the far end of the corridor, Ryan could see a cluster of kids crowded around two large pieces of paper taped to the wall. Ryan and Jessica picked up their speed.

Zeke popped out of the crowd as Ryan approached. "Hey, Ry!" he shouted. "You, me, and Miles are on the same team!"

The two boys traded high fives as Ryan made his way to the edge of the crowd. "What about Eli?" Ryan asked.

"Aaah, bad news—our big guy's with a bunch of show-offs," Zeke replied, his voice filled with disappointment.

"What do you mean, show-offs?" Drew Moyers bellowed from the wall where he stood with Eddie Wilson. "Eli's on the best team in the league," Drew called. "He's got me, Eddie, Patrick...."

Zeke turned red. He had no idea the "show-offs" were standing right there. Ryan just ignored Drew's bragging.

"Come on, Jessica," Ryan said. The two of them elbowed their way to the front of the crowd to study the rosters. Zeke and Miles stood off to the side.

INTRAMURALS — TEAM ROSTERS

North Carolina Tar Heels

Ryan Phillips
Edward Wilkowski
Jessica Abell
Nathaniel Li
Miles DuBow
Daniel Murphy
Gabriella Eisenberg
Zachary Devlin-Folty

Clemson Tigers

Johnny Fleming
Paige Vinson
Christopher Lupin
Dustin Henry
Benjamin Karesh
Tracie Czwarzik
Daniel Anderson
Michael Stamm

Duke Blue Devils

Eddie Wilson
Eli Powell
Drew Moyors
Cara Hampton
Gregory Thomas
Patrick Barrow
Wendy Reiter
Sandy Katz

Wake Forest Demon Deacons

Antoine Daniels
Nathan Harmata
Ian Will
Anne Sherman
Luiz Fernandez
Hannah Will
Ari Goldberg-Strassler
Nicholas Chu

Maryland Terrapins

Frankie Reilly
Andrew Kaplan
Mary Frances McDermott
Alex Kaess
Michael Shube
Peter Funiciello
Angela Narcho
Jacob Waldron-Kaufman

Virginia Cavaliers

Scott Hudson
Matthew Finn
Andrew Kaess
Gilbert Wiafe
Katie Noethe
Anthony Coppola
Thu Tran
Ben Garmoe

"Hey, Jessica, we're on the same team—North Carolina," Ryan exclaimed. And then he yelled over to Zeke: "You didn't tell me we got Jessica."

"What am I? ESPN SportsCenter?" Zeke said with a shrug.

"She'll help us," Miles said as Ryan nodded in agreement.

"You mean you guys will help *me*," Jessica said.

"Your whole team is going to need all the help it can get," Drew teased. Eddie laughed, and Drew added, "Because we're going to roll."

"We'll see who'll *roll* when the games start," Zeke replied.

"When do they start?" Ryan asked, looking over the rosters for a schedule.

"Tomorrow," Miles said. "There are two games every Tuesday, Wednesday, and Thursday after school."

Zeke pointed to the clump of kids in front of another large piece of paper taped on the wall. "The league schedule is down there," he said. "Every team plays twice a week for five weeks and then there are try-outs for the Sligo team."

Ryan moved a few steps down the corridor and studied the first few games of the schedule.

"Who do we play first?" Jessica asked.

"Duke at four o'clock tomorrow," Ryan said, then he looked over to Zeke. "Hey, Zeke," Ryan called. "Who's on the Duke team?"

Drew Moyers and Eddie Wilson pointed at their chests and smiled.

"We are," they said together.

FOUR

The next afternoon, Ryan tossed a shirt at Zeke, who was sitting on the boys' locker room bench lacing up his sneakers.

"What's this?" Zeke asked as Ryan continued tossing shirts to his teammates on the North Carolina intramural team.

"What does it look like?" Ryan asked impatiently. "It's a team jersey."

"They're all red!" Zeke cried in disgust.

"So what?"

"We're the North Carolina Tar Heels," Zeke protested. "They wear light blue, not red."

"What's the difference?" Ryan said. "We're not really North Carolina. Red or blue, you'll still play the same."

"Yeah, but...but...." Zeke stammered. "It's not right. Red? For North Carolina?" He shook his head and reluctantly pulled on the shirt.

Within minutes, the boys and girls of the North Carolina team were on the floor, huddled in front of their bench.

"We're going to need a captain," Jessica said.

"How about Zeke?" Ryan suggested.

"Yeah," Miles agreed and then teased, "He's good at bossing people around."

Zeke perked up and took charge. "Let's start Jessica and me as guards," he said, looking around the huddle. "Ryan, Miles, and Daniel start up front."

"Who's going to cover Drew?" Ryan asked.

"I'll take him," Jessica volunteered.

"I'll take Eddie Wilson," Ryan said.

"I'll guard Eli," Daniel Murphy said.

"Okay, Tar Heels, let's go."

As the teams lined up, Zeke poked Ryan and motioned to the stands. "Look who's here," he said. Ryan looked up and saw Coach DeCamp, the Sligo basketball coach, leaning forward on the top row and studying the action on the court.

"Who's that with him?" Ryan asked, nodding at the kid with a clipboard in his lap.

"That's Benny the Brain, the best math student in the whole school," Zeke answered.

"He keeps the statistics for Coach DeCamp. Points, rebounds, assists and all that stuff."

Zeke smiled and patted Ryan on the shoulder. "You'd better play well. Somebody's watching."

Ryan took a deep breath, shook his hands by his side, and took his position on the court. Suddenly he was very nervous.

Ryan stayed nervous. He took a pass from Zeke, faked a shot, and dribbled hard to the basket. But the ball glanced off his leg and bounced out of bounds. "Oh no!" yelled Ryan, angrily slapping his leg. He took another deep breath and hustled upcourt, sneaking a quick look at the stands. Benny the Brain was marking in his notebook. Coach DeCamp was focused on the game.

Despite a slow start, the Tar Heels hung tough. Jessica hounded Drew into a series of bad shots. Zeke zipped through the Duke defenders for twisting layups. Just before halftime, Ryan nailed two long jump shots to cut the Duke lead to three points, 19–16.

At the half, the team gulped water and Zeke barked out instructions: "Jessica, great job on defense. You got Drew all messed up, but we've gotta keep Eli and Eddie off the boards," he said. "Miles, you've got to block Eli. He's killing us."

"Hey, I'm trying," Miles shot back. "But did you notice that Eli is a lot bigger than me?"

The second half brought much of the same. The first time down the court, Drew took a wild shot for Duke that bounced high off the rim. Eli reached up over Ryan and Miles and snapped down the rebound. Then he flipped a quick jump hook off the backboard and through the net. Duke led North Carolina, 21–16.

"Nice shot, Eli. You traitor," Ryan said with a smile as the boys ran downcourt.

Eli smiled back. "Sorry, Ryan. But I'm just trying to look good for Coach DeCamp. Same as you."

North Carolina did not play well in the second half. Ryan and Zeke struggled with their shots and no one could stop Eli and Eddie from pounding the boards and scoring in close. The Duke lead stretched larger as Drew nailed three straight jump shots.

Jessica swished a pair of three-pointers for North Carolina late in the game. But Duke easily beat North Carolina, 40–28.

"You've gotta admit the best team won," Drew said to Ryan as the two teams filed off the court and headed to the locker rooms.

"You guys never would have won without Eli," Ryan said.

"Yeah," Miles said. "Eli, how can you stand playing with them?"

"I didn't have a choice," Eli said.

"Lay off him," Zeke said. "You can't choose your intramural team, and intramurals don't matter anyway. He's just trying to make the Sligo team."

Before Ryan hit the locker room, he took one last look at the stands. Benny hadn't moved. He was still writing in his notebook. Coach DeCamp was gone.

Ryan nudged Zeke. "What do you think Benny's writing?"

"He can't be writing anything good about me," Miles said, sounding tired and discouraged. "I played lousy."

Zeke turned and shouted, "Hey, Benny!"

Benny looked up, surprised to hear someone call his name.

"How much do we have to pay you to mark down some extra points and rebounds

Benny looked up, surprised
to hear someone call his name.

for us?" Zeke asked as he motioned to Ryan, Eli, Miles, and himself.

Benny smiled. "You guys don't have to worry. You did all right."

Ryan smiled for a moment too, but as he pushed through the door leading to the boys' locker room, he leaned over and whispered to Miles, "I'm not sure Benny's telling the truth. At least about me."

FIVE

The ball came flashing low and hard across the net. Ryan lunged and flicked a soft forehand that bounced high. But Eli was ready for it. He smashed a forehand shot so quickly it made Ryan's head snap back as he watched the ball zip by him.

"It's 16–9, my lead, your serve," Eli said evenly as Ryan searched for the Ping-Pong ball on the floor.

"Whew!" Miles exclaimed. "The big guy came to play today."

"You're getting pretty good at this game, Eli," Ryan said as he returned to the table.

"Just lucky." Eli smiled.

Miles put his saxophone to his lips and then paused. "Hey, where's Zeke?" he asked.

"He got detention today," Ryan said, getting ready to serve. "He said he would be late."

"What did he get detention for?" Miles asked.

"I don't know." Ryan shrugged and spun a serve to Eli.

Miles went back to playing music. Ryan and Eli returned to their game. The basement filled with sounds: Miles's saxophone, the *plick-plock* of the Ping-Pong ball, and the autumn rain beating against the windows.

Suddenly, another sound interrupted all the others. *Rap rap rat-a-tat rap.* Someone was knocking at the basement door. But no one moved to answer it. Ryan and Eli kept battling for another point and Miles kept blowing on his sax.

Rap rap! Raprapraprap! "Come on, guys, open up," Zeke called. "I know you're in there."

Ryan angled a backhand past Eli and then answered the door. "All right, all right," he said as he turned the dead bolt. "Don't break down the door."

Zeke pushed the door open and let in a wet gust of wind. "Thanks a lot for taking your time," he moaned. "In case you haven't noticed, it's raining out there." He shook his head like a wet dog trying to get dry.

Miles stopped practicing his scales. "Hey, Zeke," he asked, "who gave you detention?"

"Goldberg," Zeke replied, spitting out the name.

"What did you do?" Ryan asked.

"I didn't do anything," Zeke said as he peeled off his wet coat and tossed it on a chair. "The whole thing was totally dumb."

"Come on, Zeke," Eli said. "You must have done something to tick off Goldberg."

"I was just talking in class," Zeke said.

"Hey, what's new," Ryan said. "You're always talking in class."

"That's right," Zeke agreed, shrugging, "so why should I be punished today?"

Ryan, Eli, and Miles burst out laughing. Zeke started to laugh, too. Then he settled into a beat-up old chair and waited while Eli finished beating Ryan.

"Hey, I've got some great news for all you basketball hopefuls," Zeke said as Ryan and Eli put down their paddles.

"Is Coach DeCamp going to pick more than twelve players?" Ryan asked hopefully.

Zeke shook his head. "Nah, it's always twelve. They've only got twelve uniforms."

"So what's the good news?" Eli asked.

"Eddie Wilson is flunking math!" Zeke announced, smiling.

"So what?" Eli said, puzzled.

"So, Eddie made the team last year, and if he flunks math, he can't play this year...."

"And if he can't play," Ryan said, picking up where Zeke left off, "there's one more spot open for one of us."

"You got it!" Zeke said, pointing at Ryan. "You aren't flunking math!"

A pained look crossed Eli's face. "I don't know," he said. "It doesn't seem right—hoping someone's going to flunk so one of us can make the team."

"You want to make the team, don't you?" Zeke asked.

"Yeah, I want to make the team."

"We all want to make the team, Zeke," said Ryan. "We just don't want to make the team because someone is flunking math."

"Why not? Look at that list you made the other day," Zeke fired back as he pointed at the computer. "A whole *bunch* of kids are not going to make the Sligo team so we can make it."

Miles stopped playing in the middle of a note. "Will you guys cut it out?" he said. "What's the big deal about making the team, anyway?"

Zeke's mouth fell open. "What, are you nuts?" he blurted out. "Making the Sligo team is the biggest thing there is."

Ryan and Eli nodded in agreement.

"It's only middle school," Miles said.

"So what's that got to do with anything?" Zeke asked impatiently.

"So, Michael Jordan didn't even make his high school varsity team the first time he tried out," Miles said, smirking.

"No way!" shouted Zeke, Ryan, and Eli all at once.

"Michael's the best!" said Zeke.

"He always was," Ryan added confidently, then paused. "Wasn't he?"

"Not always," said Miles, still grinning. "He got cut in his sophomore year and had to play on the junior varsity."

"Wait. I did hear something about that," Zeke said. "But he must have been sick or hurt or something during tryouts."

"No, he just wasn't good enough," Miles said.

"So what did he do?" Eli asked.

"He practiced, got bigger, got better."

"A lot better." Ryan laughed. "So some high school coach didn't think Michael Jordan was good enough for varsity? That coach must be feeling pretty dumb."

"How do you know so much about Michael Jordan, anyway?" Zeke asked.

"I read a book about him." Miles went back to playing his saxophone. The other boys were silent as Miles's slow, sad song filled the basement.

After a few moments Ryan broke the silence and said what each of the boys was thinking. "Man, if Michael Jordan got cut from his high school varsity team, I guess *anybody* can get cut from a team."

"We'll make it," Zeke said quickly. "Don't worry."

"How can you be so sure?" Ryan asked.

"Because we're all going to play really well and Benny the Brain is going to take down every point."

"Yeah, but are we all going to play better than Michael Jordan did?" Eli asked.

SIX

Ms. Monnier, the referee, held up two fingers as she handed the ball to the Clemson player standing on the foul line. "Two shots," she said. "Relax on the first one."

Ryan was standing along the foul line, waiting for the Clemson player to take his first shot. Ryan leaned over, tugged at his basketball shorts, and glanced up into the stands. Coach DeCamp and Benny were sitting in their usual spots for intramural games, on the last row.

I hope Benny is taking good notes today, Ryan thought, happily adding up his points, rebounds, and assists for the game so far. *This game has got to help me make the team. We've only got a few more games left.*

The player's first shot bounced off the rim. Ryan looked up at the scoreboard.

HOME   VISITOR

UNC Tar Heels   Clemson Tigers

3 6   03:00   4   2 2

PERIOD

The Tar Heels were safely ahead, 36–22, with only three minutes to play. Ryan glanced up again at Coach DeCamp and Benny as he leaned in, ready for the rebound. *Maybe I can score a few more points before this game's over,* he thought.

The second foul shot bounced around the rim and fell through. Zeke dribbled the ball past half court and snapped a pass to Jessica on the right wing. She faked left and drove to the right, slipping by her defender. Another Clemson player moved over to stop her. But at the last instant, Jessica flicked a pass to Ryan, who was waiting in the corner. He quickly put the ball up and watched it rip through the net.

All smiles, Ryan ran back on defense, slapping hands with Zeke and Jessica.

"Good pass, Jessica," he said. "Hands-up defense."

When Clemson missed another shot, Miles grabbed the rebound and flicked a quick pass to Zeke. The Tar Heel leader passed to Ryan, who was racing upcourt. Ryan dribbled past the Clemson defender and scored on an easy layup.

The teams traded baskets in the final minute. Jessica swished a long jumper just as the buzzer sounded. North Carolina had romped to a 44–25 win.

"All right, Tar Heels!" Zeke shouted after the teams had shaken hands.

"That really helps our record," Miles said.

"Four wins, four losses," Ryan responded. "Not too bad."

"Man, that was our best game of the season," Zeke said, still beaming.

"It was definitely Ryan's best game," Jessica said as the team moved slowly toward the locker rooms. "And Miles must have had a gazillion rebounds."

Ryan glanced up at the stands again. Coach DeCamp was gone, but Benny was there marking in his notebook.

Zeke grabbed Ryan playfully around the neck. "Hey, Benny!" Zeke shouted.

Benny looked up.

"Did you get all of my man Michael Jordan's—I mean Ryan's—points down in your notebook?" Zeke yelled. "I know it was tough because he got so many."

Benny smiled. "Don't worry, I got them all," he said, tapping his pencil on his notebook. "All fourteen of them."

Halfway down the steps to the boys' locker room, Ryan, Zeke, and Miles ran into Drew Moyers in uniform, heading to the gym. "How'd you do?" Drew asked.

"Won big time," Zeke announced proudly, "44–25."

"Who'd you play?"

"Clemson," Ryan said.

Drew nodded, then said, "Hey, Zeke, can I talk to you for a minute?"

Zeke looked at Ryan and Miles. Ryan, sensing they were not wanted, nudged Miles. "We'll see you later, Zeke," he said.

"What does Drew want with Zeke?" Miles asked as the boys pushed open the door to the locker room.

"I don't know," Ryan answered, still thinking about the game.

A few minutes later, Zeke joined Ryan and Miles in the locker room.

"What did Drew want?" Miles asked.

"He wanted me to play in a three-on-three basketball tournament in the city this weekend with some guys who made last year's Sligo team," Zeke said as he yanked his sweaty red shirt over his head. "He said they could use another guard."

"Sounds cool," Ryan said. "What did you say?"

Zeke shook his head. "I told him no."

"Why?" Miles asked.

"I'd rather beat those guys than play with them," Zeke said, pulling a piece of paper from the pocket of his shorts and unfolding it. "And anyway, I told him we've already got a team."

"We've already got a team?" Ryan repeated. "Who's 'we'?"

"You, me, Eli, and Miles," Zeke said with a big smile. "I think we'll make a pretty good team."

"Maybe, but we haven't signed up for the tournament," Miles said.

"This says we can fax in our application by tomorrow and pay the money on Saturday before we play," Zeke said, holding up the paper.

Ryan grabbed the paper from Zeke, who sat down and began to unlace his sneakers. Miles peered over Ryan's shoulder and the boys read the paper together. "Hey, we've gotta choose a name for our team," Miles said.

"Did Drew tell you the name of his team?" Ryan asked.

"The Chosen Few," Zeke said.

Ryan rolled his eyes. "Those guys think they're so great just because they made the Sligo team last year," Ryan said. "I hope we get to play them in this tournament. Then they'll be calling themselves The *Rejected* Few."

"Okay, but what about our name? How 'bout The Chosen Too?" Zeke smiled.

"We need a name that really fits us," Miles said slowly. "What do you think of when you think of us?"

"I think of playing basketball, playing football, playing Ping-Pong, hanging out at Ryan's...." Zeke started.

Ryan laughed and then snapped his fingers. "Hey, I've got it!"

Zeke and Miles looked at Ryan and waited.

"What you said, Zeke. We're always hanging out in my basement, right? We're the Cellar Dwellers!"

SEVEN

Early Saturday morning, Ryan's stepfather pulled the car up to the curb at the train station. Ryan, Zeke, Eli, and Miles, all dressed in basketball gear, hopped out. "Be careful," Max said. "Call when you get back to the station and your mom or I will come get you."

"Okay," Ryan said.

"Do you know when you'll be back?"

Ryan smiled. "It depends on how many games we win."

"Well, good luck, guys," Max called out as he drove away.

"Hey, hurry up!" Eli shouted. "A train is coming."

The four boys pushed their fare cards through the machine and sprinted up the escalator. They tumbled into the train just as the doors were closing. The train was almost empty. Eli and Zeke sat on one side of the aisle and Miles and Ryan sat on the other.

"Hey, Zeke," Eli said, tossing the basketball over to Ryan, "what are the rules for these games, anyway?"

Zeke pulled the wrinkled application out of his basketball shorts and read from the piece of paper. "It's three-on-three half court. Games to twenty points."

"Do baskets count for two points?" Ryan asked, flipping the ball back across the aisle to Eli.

Zeke nodded, still reading. "Foul shots are one point each, just like in regular basketball. A team has to clear the ball past the three-point line after every possession."

"Are there three-pointers?" Ryan asked.

"Yeah, but let's not go crazy shooting three-pointers," Zeke warned. "Let's try to work it in to Eli for some closer shots."

"Can you foul out of the game?" Miles asked.

Zeke nodded and held up three fingers. "Three fouls and you're out of the game."

"You'd better watch the fouls, Eli," Ryan advised. "We don't want you fouling out. You're our only big guy."

Zeke, Eli, and Miles kept talking, but Ryan began to stare out the window. The houses and lawns of the boys' hometown drifted by and slowly gave way to the tall buildings and concrete of the city.

"This is our stop," Zeke said, startling Ryan, who was deep in thought.

The boys scrambled off the train into the waking downtown streets. The morning sunshine fell between the tall buildings, creating a checkerboard of light and darkness on the city scene.

"Which way are we going, Zeke?" Ryan asked, walking quickly to keep pace with the others.

"I think it's this way."

"Wait. Listen," said Eli, stopping suddenly. "Hear that?"

It was the distant sound of basketballs pounding on pavement.

"Over there," Zeke said, pointing.

The boys broke into a brisk jog with Zeke leading the way, dribbling as he jogged. They turned a corner and saw a long city block that had been transformed into a basketball extravaganza. More than thirty hoops lined the streets and players of all ages were practicing their half-court games. The air was filled with basketballs and basketball chatter.

Thunk. A ball hit the rim on a nearby court. "Our ball!" A kid ran right in front of Ryan, chasing the out-of-bounds ball. The Cellar Dwellers passed another court. A tall boy launched the ball toward the net. *Swish.* "You just can't stop my jumper!" he shouted. To the left, a group of boys exchanged high fives and a small crowd cheered. "Who's got next?" one of the boys asked.

Ryan and the other Dwellers took their place in line at the registration table tucked inside a large billowy tent. It only took a few minutes for them to move to the front of the line.

"Team name?" the tournament official asked as Ryan handed over their money.

"The Cellar Dwellers."

"Okay," the official said, moving his finger down a long piece of paper. "You're on Court 18 in fifteen minutes against the Downtowners."

Ryan elbowed Eli and motioned to a large chart hanging in back of the table.

"Look, if we beat the Downtowners," Ryan said, "we may get to play the Chosen Few."

Eli smiled. "Let's worry about finding Court 18 and beating the Downtowners first."

3-ON-3 TOURNAMENT

7th and 8th Grades

```
The Cellar Dwellers ─┐
                     ├─┐
The Downtowners    ─┐ │
                      │ ├─┐
The Chosen Few     ─┐ │   │
                     ├─┘   │
Henry's Hoopsters  ─┘       ├───
                            │
The Court Jesters  ─┐       │
                     ├─┐     │
Skywalkers         ─┘ │     │
                      ├─┘
Kings of the Court ─┐ │
                     ├─┘
Dunkmasters        ─┘
```

The Downtowners were already on the court warming up when the Cellar Dwellers arrived. The Cellar Dwellers started throwing in a couple of practice shots. But after just a few minutes, the referee blew his whistle and said, "Okay, let's go."

The Downtowners jumped to a 6–0 lead before Ryan and his buddies could get

45

warmed up. But the Cellar Dwellers didn't quit. Zeke drove hard to the basket and flipped a pass to Ryan for an open 15-foot jump shot. *Swish.*

"Great shot!" Eli yelled. "Come on, Dwellers, play D."

Eli rebounded a miss by the Downtowners and cleared a pass to Zeke out in three-point territory. Zeke wasted no time and put up the ball. It bounced off the rim, but Eli was right there. He snatched the rebound and tossed a quick hook shot up and in.

"Yes!" Zeke yelled. Then he waved Miles over from the bench. "Hey, Miles, come in for Ryan."

Ryan sat down on a plastic chair at the edge of the court. "Come on, Dwellers!" he shouted. "Let's go!"

The teams traded baskets. Then Zeke drove in with a twisting layup. *Phweeet!* The referee's whistle blew just as the ball fell through the net.

"Basket is good!" the referee called. "One foul shot."

Zeke stood at the foul line and pointed to Ryan. "Ryan, come in for Eli," he said. "And, Eli, you come in for me in a couple of minutes."

Zeke's foul shot rolled around the rim and in. The Cellar Dwellers led the game for the first time, 9–8.

But the lead slipped away. When Eli was on the bench, the Cellar Dwellers had trouble rebounding. With Zeke out, the Cellar Dwellers had trouble handling the ball. Within minutes, it was the Downtowners game, 18–13. Two more points for the Downtowners and the Cellar Dwellers would be on the train heading back home.

"Time out!" Zeke shouted from the sidelines.

"Come on, we've gotta come back," Zeke said as the boys huddled.

"You'd better come in for me, Zeke," Miles gasped, tapping his chest and trying to catch his breath.

"Come on, guys," someone called. "You've gotta win so we can beat you next game." The Cellar Dwellers turned to see Drew Moyers. He was standing next to Eddie Wilson, Patrick Barrow, and another guy at the side of the court and he had a big grin on his face.

"How'd you guys do?" Zeke asked him.

"Won 20–15," Drew answered.

Zeke turned his attention back to the huddle. "Come on, we've gotta win so we get a chance at the Chosen Few. Okay, I'll drive to the basket. Ryan, you spot up for the three-pointer. Let's go." ·

The boys clapped together as Zeke, Ryan, and Eli ran onto the court. The first chance he got, Zeke drove hard to the hoop and whipped a pass to Ryan. The ball barely touched Ryan's hands before he sent up a jumper past a leaping defender.

Swish! Three-pointer! 18–16!

Zeke stole a pass and found Eli underneath the basket for a quick bucket. Tie ball game! 18–18!

"Come on, Dwellers!" Ryan yelled, his heart pounding. "Defense."

The Downtowners guard sneaked a bounce pass to their big guy near the basket. He went up strong, and Eli went up with him, stretching for the block. But Eli's hand missed the ball and hit the Downtowner on his wrist.

Phweeet! "Foul," the referee called. "Two shots."

Ryan stood helplessly along the foul line. His shoulders slumped as the Downtowners center got ready to shoot.

If he makes both shots, we're out of the tournament, Ryan thought.

The first shot ripped through the net. 19–18.

Please miss it, Ryan pleaded as the second shot spun to the hoop.

The ball bounced high off the rim and Eli snapped down the rebound, shooting a quick pass to Zeke just beyond the three-point arc.

"Ryan!" Zeke called as he faked a pass and drove to the basket. He floated a running right-hander up to the rim.

Eli and Ryan rushed to the basket expecting a rebound, but the ball bounced softly around the rim and plopped in.

The Cellar Dwellers had won, 20–19!

Ryan turned and saw Miles pumping his fist in the air as he ran happily onto the court. Behind Miles, standing along the sidelines, Drew Moyers and the Chosen Few were smiling.

EIGHT

The Cellar Dwellers hustled back to the registration tent to find out where and when their next game was. "Hey, here we are," said Miles. "We're playing the Chosen Few on Court 23 in 10 minutes."

"Ten minutes!" Ryan repeated. "What about a rest?"

"Quit whining," Zeke said. "That's plenty of time. Let's go."

The boys dashed past a string of makeshift courts filled with three-on-three games in full swing—whistles were blowing, kids were yelling, and balls were flying. "Hey, that must be Court 23," shouted Eli as he spotted Drew and his team warming up on a court in the distance.

The boys picked up their speed. "Okay," Ryan said, half-yelling to be heard above the whistles, cheers, and pounding basketballs. "Who's covering who?"

"I'd better take Eddie," Eli called out as he jogged alongside Ryan. "He's their biggest guy."

Zeke and Miles were keeping pace right behind Ryan and Eli. "Ryan, you want to take Drew?" Zeke called back.

"What? I can't hear you."

"Do you want to take Drew?" Zeke repeated a little louder.

"Okay," Ryan said, slowing his pace as they reached Court 23. "But I wish we had Jessica. She did a great job covering him in intramurals."

"Just don't let him drive on you," Miles suggested, a little out of breath.

"Yeah, make him shoot from outside," Zeke said, as the boys came to a stop. "He thinks he's a better shooter than he is."

"What if he starts hitting his outside shot?" Ryan asked.

"Then we lose," Zeke replied, dribbling his ball onto the court. The boys took a handful of hurried shots and then heard the starting whistle.

"I guess I don't have to tell you," Zeke said as the boys huddled at the side of the court, "but if we lose this one, we'll never hear the end of it."

"Yeah," Ryan said with a sly grin. "But if we win, *they'll* never hear the end of it."

The two teams took the court, shook hands, and played as if more than just bragging rights were at stake. Every possession was a battle and every basket was hard-won.

Drew Moyers drained his first two jump shots and put the Chosen Few ahead early, 4–0.

"Don't worry, he'll start missing," Zeke whispered to Ryan.

Sure enough, Drew cooled off and the Cellar Dwellers came back. Zeke kept slipping the ball to Eli, who powered it in for baskets. When the Chosen Few started double-teaming Eli, he began rocketing the ball to Zeke and Ryan. The Dwellers sharpshooters knocked down jump shot after jump shot and pushed the Dwellers ahead of the Chosen Few, 12–10.

"Time out!" shouted Eddie Wilson, pushing his hands high in the air in the form of a *T.*

The Cellar Dwellers joined Miles on the sidelines. He slapped high fives with Ryan and Eli.

"Quit celebrating!" Zeke warned. "We're only up by a basket. They want to win as much as we do. We've got to keep playing hard. They're not going to let up."

"This is a great game," Miles said, looking around the makeshift city-street basketball court.

"Yeah," Zeke agreed, but quickly added, "let's make sure we win it."

Ryan, Zeke, and Eli walked back onto the court. Their hair was wet with sweat and their damp, stained shirts clung to their skin.

The game stayed close. The Cellar Dwellers were leading 16–14 when Zeke missed a jump shot and tall Eddie Wilson snapped down the rebound. He instantly got the ball to Drew in three-point territory. Drew faked a long shot and bounced the ball back to Eddie, who leaped high with a quick shot. Eli strained to block it.

Phweeet! The referee's whistled sounded as the ball glanced off the backboard and through the net. "The basket is good. The foul is on the big guy. One shot."

As Eddie took his place at the foul line, the high-school kid at the scorer's table called, "That's three fouls on the big guy for the Cellar Dwellers. He's out of the game. They need a substitute."

"Aaaaargh," Eli moaned as he tossed his head back in despair.

Miles rushed in to replace him.

The Cellar Dwellers quickly huddled in the middle of the court.

"You've got to cover Eddie," Ryan said to Miles.

"Me? But Eddie's too big for me," Miles blurted out.

"You can cover him," Zeke argued. "Just stay with him. The game's to twenty. We just need two more baskets."

"All right," Miles said with new determination. "Let's go."

Eli took his place on the sidelines, wiped his face with a towel, and threw it angrily on the street. "Come on, Dwellers, we're still in it!" he yelled as he paced back and forth.

Eddie sank the free throw to put the Chosen Few ahead, 17–16. On the next possession, the Cellar Dwellers passed the ball around, looking for a good shot. The Chosen Few, energized by their one-point lead, hounded the Cellar Dwellers and shouted to each other.

"Big D! Big D!"

"No shooters. No shooters."

Ryan could feel the game slipping away. *I've gotta make something happen,* he thought. "Over here," he called to Zeke, who flipped him the ball on the right wing. Ryan drove left and threw up an off-balance jump shot just over Drew's fingers. The ball touched off the rim, hit the backboard, and fell through. Now it was the Cellar Dwellers turn to shout.

"Great shot!"

"All right, Ryan."

"Play defense!"

The Chosen Few quickly tried to get the ball to Eddie underneath, but Miles reached in and tapped the ball loose. The ball was headed out of bounds but Miles dove head-long after it and slapped it to Ryan. Miles skidded across the asphalt but Ryan got the ball.

Before the Chosen Few could recover and set up their defense, Ryan threaded a pass to Zeke, who was breaking to the hoop. Zeke went in for an easy layup.

The Cellar Dwellers had won, 20–17!

The Chosen Few were stunned. They mumbled "good game" and exchanged weak handshakes with the Cellar Dwellers, then walked off into the crowd.

*Ryan drove left and threw up an off-balance
jump shot just over Drew's fingers.*

The Cellar Dwellers lost their next game to the Court Jesters, but stayed to watch a couple more games. Then they caught a crowded train home. As the train rumbled forward, the great buildings of the city fell away in the distance.

"No way we should have lost that last game to the Court Jesters," Zeke said angrily. "They weren't that good."

"I just got tired of getting all the rebounds," Eli teased.

"Quit complaining. We won the big game," Miles said, picking at the scab of dried blood on his right knee.

The four friends sat silently, smiling with the memory of beating the Chosen Few.

"You know, I think beating those guys is going to be better than making the Sligo team," Ryan said, still smiling.

Zeke shook his head firmly. "Nothing is going to be better than making the team," he said.

NINE

Ryan looked up as the football sailed high against the November sky. He ran as fast as he could but could only watch helplessly as the football flew past him, hit the ground, and somersaulted away. He turned and put his hands on his hips as the other team celebrated around him.

"We won that game!" shouted Dustin Henry. "Do you guys want to play another?"

"Nah," Ryan said. "It's getting late." He walked toward Eli and Miles. "Do you guys just want to come to my house?" he asked.

"Sure," they replied.

Miles picked up his saxophone case and walked slowly across the big open field with Ryan and Eli. "We were pretty bad today," he said.

"We didn't have our quarterback," Ryan said, tossing the football in the air.

"Hey, sorry I can't throw like Zeke," Eli said. "Where is he, anyway?"

"In detention," Miles said. "Goldberg got him again for wisecracking in class."

"Man, Zeke must pay rent in the detention room," Ryan laughed. "He's there all the time."

The three friends walked through Ryan's front door.

"Is that you, Ry?" Max called from the back of the house.

"Yeah. Eli and Miles are with me. We're going downstairs."

"Okay."

The boys descended the narrow steps and took up their usual spots in the basement. Miles sat on the edge of a chair practicing his scales while Ryan and Eli smacked the Ping-Pong ball back and forth.

"What time is tomorrow's basketball tryout?" Eli asked.

"Three o'clock. Right after school," Ryan said.

"Is that going to be the only tryout?" Miles asked.

"No, Miles. Wake up. There's another one on Thursday," Ryan said as he smacked a forehand into the net.

"Oh, yeah. *Then* Coach DeCamp picks the team."

"Right." Ryan nodded as Eli's serve whistled by.

"Come on, Ryan," Eli said impatiently. "Get your head in the game. I'm already up 11–4. You'd better play better than this in tryouts."

Just as Ryan served, the boys heard a knock on the basement door. "Come on, guys. Let me in," Zeke called.

"Will you get the door, Miles?" Ryan said. "I'm busy playing."

"Why me?" Miles protested. "I'm playing too."

Zeke kept knocking louder and louder. Eli's next shot skidded past Ryan and onto the floor.

"All right. All right," Ryan called, moving toward the door. "Don't break the door down."

Zeke rushed in, swinging his backpack off his shoulder. "Man, it's about time," he said.

"Goldberg give you detention again?" Miles asked.

"Yeah, so what?"

"So you missed a touch football game at the park," Ryan said.

"How did you do without me?" Zeke asked, flopping into a chair.

"We lost."

Zeke flashed a wide, satisfied smile. "Guess you guys needed your star quarterback. Hey, guess who I saw in detention today?"

"Who?"

"Benny the Brain!"

"No way," Ryan said. "The teachers love Benny. He couldn't get detention if he tried."

"Okay, so he wasn't really in detention," Zeke admitted. "But he was in the room helping Eddie Wilson with his math."

"How's Eddie doing?" Ryan asked nervously.

Zeke shook his head. "Benny will have him doing college-level math before long. Believe me, Eddie isn't going to flunk math."

"So he'll be able to play on the team," Ryan said, picturing another name appearing on the final team list.

"Yeah, but guess what Benny gave me?" Zeke said, reaching into his backpack.

"What?"

"The final stats for the intramural league."

Miles stopped playing the saxophone, and Ryan and Eli put their paddles down. When Zeke smoothed the sheet of paper on the Ping-Pong table, the four boys studied the columns of numbers as if they were the secret to a lost treasure.

INTRAMURAL STATISTICS

Scoring Average		Rebounding Average	
Antoine Daniels	15.3	Eli Powell	8.4
Eddie Wilson	14.0	Matthew Finn	7.8
Alex Kaess	12.9	Johnny Fleming	6.5
Drew Moyers	12.4	Gilbert Wiafe	6.4
Ian Will	12.0	Eddie Wilson	5.9

Assists per Game		Shooting Percentage	
Luiz Fernandez	5.2	Nathan Harmata	48.6
Edward Zilkowski	5.0	Jessica Abell	47.5
Patrick Barrow	4.6	Eli Powell	47.1
Frankie Reilly	4.4	Eddie Wilson	46.4
Scott Hudson	3.0	Andrew Kaess	44.4

Steals per Game		Free Throw Percentage	
Edward Zilkowski	3.0	Jessica Abell	91.7
Luiz Fernandez	1.8	Andrew Kaess	85.0
Antoine Daniels	1.6	Nathan Harmata	83.8
Nicholas Chu	1.6	Daniel Anderson	75.0
Eddie Wilson	1.3	Hannah Will	71.4

"Hey, look who the rebound king is," Miles exclaimed, punching Eli on the shoulder. "You've got it made for sure, big guy."

"Drew's one of the leading scorers," Ryan said, pointing to one of the columns.

"He ought to be," Zeke said. "He takes a million shots and never passes to anybody else."

Ryan kept studying the columns, silently calculating his chances to make the team.

"I'm not on any of the lists," he said sadly.

"Benny just printed out the leaders," Zeke said. "You probably barely missed some of the lists."

"Yeah, but only the top guys are going to make the team," Ryan said.

"Hey, don't worry," Zeke said. "You'll make the team."

"Doesn't look like it to me," Ryan said, looking over the intramural statistics.

"Hey, if Ryan doesn't make it," Miles said, picking up his saxophone, "there's no way I'm going to make it."

"You guys will both make it," Zeke insisted.

"How do you figure?" Ryan asked.

"You guys are good passers, you play good defense, you can score, and...." Zeke paused dramatically.

"And what?" Ryan asked.

"You've still got the tryouts for the team!" Zeke said as he threw his arm around Ryan's shoulder. "And both of you are going to have great tryouts."

TEN

The shot felt perfect as it left Ryan's hand. He watched it soar to the basket. But it angled off its path as a shower of basketballs bounced about the rim, bumping and fighting each other for a way to the net. Ryan grabbed a bouncing rebound and looked around. Clusters of kids hoping to make the team were practicing their jump shots at the six baskets around the gym.

Ryan quietly sized up the kids to figure out his own chance of making the team. *They'll make it,* Ryan thought as he watched the Chosen Few and some hotshot eighth graders toss up shots. *No way they'll make it,* he thought, spying a group of nervous seventh graders at the far end of the floor.

"Think there are twelve kids in this gym better than you?" Zeke asked, walking up to Ryan.

"I guess we'll find out," Ryan replied.

Just then, Coach DeCamp came striding into the gym, a clipboard in his hand and a whistle around his neck.

Phweeet!

"All right," he said in a booming voice. "I want everybody to line up against the wall according to height."

The boys moved slowly to the end of the gym and arranged themselves into a long line. Ryan stood almost exactly in the middle, next to Miles. Ryan looked down the line to his left and saw Zeke standing as tall and straight as he could at the shorter end of the line. Then he looked to his right and elbowed Miles. "Hey, look," he said. "Eli is the second-tallest kid trying out. He'll make it easy."

"All right, count off one through five, starting at the end of the line," Coach DeCamp ordered.

Ryan looked to his left as the boys started calling out numbers. "One!" he shouted when his turn came.

When the last kid had counted off, Coach DeCamp continued calling out instructions: "All right, I want all the number ones to line up here at the end of the court. This is your starting line." Ryan and six other players stepped forward.

"Basketball is a game of speed and quickness," the coach said as he paced the sidelines. "So I want to see how fast each of you can move."

Ryan eyed the other boys on the line and shook his legs to loosen his muscles.

"I want you to run, touch the floor there, where that red tape is," he said, pointing at the tape eight feet inside the court, "then come back and touch the starting line, run out and touch the blue tape near the foul line, run back and touch the starting line again, and finally run and touch the green tape just beyond the foul line and back to the starting line. Understood?"

The seven boys nodded. Ryan took a deep breath and crouched down, ready to run.

"On your mark. Get set. Go!"

Ryan bolted, stopped just short of the red tape, reached down, touched it, and dashed back to the starting line and out to the blue tape. He could hear Miles, Eli, and Zeke cheering above all the others as he ran.

"Come on, Ryan, move it."

"Get the lead out!"

Ryan flashed across the finish line a half step in front of his group. He was breathing hard, but when he saw Coach DeCamp making a mark in his notebook, Ryan smiled to himself. He slapped a satisfied high five with Miles as he took his place in line.

"Good job," Miles said.

"Next group, step up to the line," Coach DeCamp called.

"Good luck," Ryan said as Miles stepped up to the line.

More than an hour later, Ryan was bent over and breathing hard after another series of drills. Coach DeCamp had put the boys through their paces. Three-player full-court weaves. Fast-break drills. Layups. Foul shots.

Ryan angrily smacked his leg, thinking about the foul shots he had missed. He knew every one of those misses was marked down in the coach's notebook.

Phweeet! Coach DeCamp's whistle shrieked. "All right, we've got time for a couple of quick scrimmages," he called. "Let's have teams one and two on the floor."

The boys on those teams ambled onto the floor as the coach barked orders. "Team one, play skins—shirts off. Man-to-man defense. I'll call fouls. Skins' ball."

Ryan pulled his damp shirt over his head. He tossed it to Zeke, who was standing at the side of the court. "Go get 'em, Ryan!" Zeke yelled.

Ryan ran downcourt, glanced at Coach DeCamp, and thought, *I don't have much time to impress him. I'd better score quick.*

Ryan popped out and took a pass on the left wing. He pivoted toward the basket. Andrew Kaplan was in his face, guarding him closely. No one was open. *Might as well try to score,* Ryan thought. Ryan faked toward the middle of the floor and Andrew took a half step back. That was enough. Ryan darted to his left, angling past Andrew to the basket. The shirts' center came over to block the shot, but Ryan leaped, sliding by the center and under the basket. At the last moment, he spun a right-handed scoop shot against the backboard. The ball glanced off the glass and fell through the net. Ryan's buddies went wild.

"All right, Ryan!"

"What a shot!"

"Score one for the Dwellers!"

Ryan ran back on defense, beaming. He glanced at the sideline. Coach DeCamp was writing in his notebook.

The ball glanced off the glass and fell through the net.

ELEVEN

"Man, did you see the look on Andrew Kaplan's face when Ryan hit that shot?" Zeke said in amazement as the boys sat around Ryan's basement the next afternoon.

"Who wants to play Ping-Pong?" Ryan asked, grabbing a paddle off the table.

"I'll play," Eli answered.

A late November rain drummed against the windows. Miles licked the reed of his saxophone and began playing.

Zeke kept talking. "I mean, Kaplan's jaw was *on the floor,*" he said. He cupped his hands around his mouth so he would sound like a sports announcer. "Ryan Phillips leaps, spins, off the glass for the deuce!" Zeke dropped his hands from his mouth, jumped on a chair, and imitated Ryan's circus shot from the day before.

"Hey, get off the chair," Ryan scolded. "My mom and Max don't want us jumping on furniture down here."

Zeke flopped down, hanging his feet over the side of the chair. "You made the team with that one move, Ryan. I know it," said Zeke, wagging a finger at his buddy.

"I'm not so sure," Ryan replied with a grunt as he drilled a forehand past Eli. "It was the only basket I scored in the scrimmage."

Zeke waved his hand as if shooing a fly away.

"Believe me, it's the only basket Coach DeCamp will remember," Zeke argued. "It was the best shot of the day."

"Hey, I get next," Miles said, nodding at the Ping-Pong table.

"No way! I got next," Zeke protested. "They're playing to see who'll get the chance to play me for the championship."

"Since when are *you* champ?" Miles squealed in disbelief.

"Since forever."

Ryan stood with his hands pressed on the table. "Zeke, you've hardly played the last two weeks. You spent most of your time in detention with Goldberg," he said sharply. "There's no way you're the champ." Ryan smacked the ball over the net to Eli.

"What do you mean?" Zeke argued. "Nobody's beaten me in the last two weeks, so I'm still champ."

"Forget it, Zeke," Ryan said, never taking his eye off the back-and-forth of the Ping-Pong ball.

"All right. All right," Zeke said. He tossed a few darts glumly at the dartboard but suddenly cheered up. "Hey, how about a game of doubles?" he asked. "Me and Ryan against Eli and Miles."

Eli laughed. "Zeke, why is it that you only want to play doubles when you're the one waiting to play?" He sliced the ball across the table to Ryan. "Forget it. You play after Miles."

Zeke plopped down in the chair with his arms crossed, looking like a kid who had been told there was no dessert. But he soon brightened.

"Hey, Ryan, where's that list you made a couple weeks ago?" he asked. "You know, the one of all the players trying out for the team."

"It's somewhere near the computer," Ryan answered, waving a paddle toward the back of the basement as he waited for Eli to serve.

Zeke rooted around on the top of the desk and returned to his chair with a wrinkled sheet of paper and a pen.

"How did Gilbert Wiafe do in the first try-out?" he asked, looking at the list.

"Okay. Not great," Ryan said as he watched the Ping-Pong ball catch the edge of the table near Eli and spin cockeyed toward the wall. "It's 20–14. My lead," Ryan said happily. "Game point."

Eli spun a serve to Ryan. Ryan sliced the ball low over the net and it skidded in tiny bounces to Eli. Ryan raised his hands high in the air. "The new champion," he announced.

Eli tossed his paddle to Miles. "You'd better be ready," he warned Miles. "Ryan is hot. Real hot."

Eli sat on the arm of Zeke's chair and peered over his shoulder. "What are you doing?" he asked Zeke.

"Checking off who's going to make the team," Zeke said.

"Isn't it kind of early for that?" Ryan said. "We've still got one more tryout."

"You watch," Zeke said confidently. "I'll pick all twelve. Hey, how did 'Legs' Funiciello do?"

"Lousy," Miles said. "He couldn't shoot and finished last in the quickness drill. He's gone."

Ryan and Miles volleyed for serve to start their game. The ball clicked back and forth in a familiar rhythm.

"What are the check marks for?" Eli asked, still peering over Zeke's shoulder.

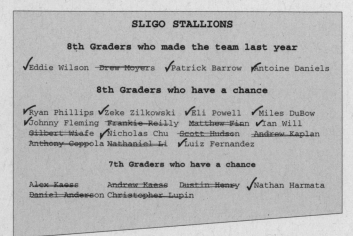

SLIGO STALLIONS

8th Graders who made the team last year

✓Eddie Wilson ~~Drew Moyers~~ ✓Patrick Barrow ✓Antoine Daniels

8th Graders who have a chance

✓Ryan Phillips ✓Zeke Zilkowski ✓Eli Powell ✓Miles DuBow
✓Johnny Fleming ~~Frankie Reilly~~ ~~Matthew Finn~~ ✓Ian Will
~~Gilbert Wiafe~~ ✓Nicholas Chu ~~Scott Hudson~~ ~~Andrew Kaplan~~
~~Anthony Coppola~~ ~~Nathaniel Li~~ ✓Luiz Fernandez

7th Graders who have a chance

~~Alex Kaess~~ ~~Andrew Kaess~~ ~~Dustin Henry~~ ✓Nathan Harmata
~~Daniel Anderson~~ ~~Christopher Lupin~~

"They're the guys I figure are going to make the team. I'm crossing out the guys who don't have a chance."

"You crossed out Drew Moyers. He's a big scorer," Eli protested.

"He's a gunner," Zeke insisted. "He must take a million shots a game. And most of them are dumb shots."

"What about Dustin Henry?"

74

"He's a seventh grader."

"The coach is going to keep some seventh graders," Ryan reminded Zeke. "And Dustin's good."

"If you don't like my list, make your own." Zeke stood up, held the paper high in the air, and announced, "I proclaim these twelve players to be this year's Sligo basketball team."

The four boys stood at the side of the table and studied the list. "I wish you were the coach, Zeke," Ryan said.

"You watch." Zeke nodded. "This will be the team. I know how to pick them."

"You really think all four of us will make the team?" Miles asked.

"Sure," Zeke said and pointed to Eli. "This guy's a shoo-in."

"I don't know why you say that," Eli protested. "The coach could cut anybody."

"Yeah, but you're tall," Zeke said. "Did you see where the coach stood when he talked to the team? Down near all the tall guys. I could barely see him because he was standing so far away from my end of the line."

"Okay, Eli makes the team because he's tall," Miles said. "But what about the rest of us?"

"Don't worry," Zeke answered. "In a couple of days we're all going to be teammates."

No one spoke. The rain drumming against the windows was the only sound in the room.

Ryan looked from side to side at his friends and finally said, "Well, we've got one more chance to make sure it happens."

TWELVE

"Count off one to five, just like on Tuesday," Coach DeCamp called out on Thursday afternoon. "And hurry up. We've got a lot of scrimmages to play."

The boys in line began to count off.

"One...two...three...."

Ryan had noticed that the line was a little shorter than on Tuesday. Some of the players had given up their dream of making the Sligo team and stayed home. *Good,* Ryan thought. *That just gives me a better chance of making the team.*

"Four...five.... One...."

"Two," Ryan called out and, as the counting off continued, he looked down the line to see who else would be on team two.

"Four...five.... One...."

"Two," Drew Moyers called out.

Oh no, not him, Ryan said to himself. *I won't*

get any chances to score with that hotshot on the team. He never passes to anyone.

Phweeet! The coach blew hard on the whistle and all the boys snapped to attention. "Let's mix it up today," he said. "Let's have team two and team four on the floor."

The boys walked onto the court as Coach DeCamp held the ball over his head and shouted instructions.

"Team two is in shirts. Team four in skins. Man-to-man defense. Shirts' ball. Benny, keep track of the time."

Benny nodded from his perch in the stands. The coach snapped a bounce pass to Chris Lupin, who passed to Drew Moyers.

Ryan hustled down the court. He popped open on the left wing, hoping for a pass. But Drew dribbled by a defender and drove to the basket. He threw up a running right-handed shot that bounced wildly off the rim.

Away from the basket, Ryan had no chance for a rebound. He raced back on defense. "Come on, Drew!" he shouted. "Pass the ball around."

But the first play was just the beginning. The shirts' team did not play well. Passes bounced too low. Shots were hurried and off the mark.

Finally, Ryan caught a good pass on the wing. He was desperate to score and show Coach DeCamp what he could do. He faked left, dipped his shoulder, and darted to the basket. Gary Day, the skins' team center, reached to block Ryan's shot but his hand caught Ryan's wrist instead.

Phweeet! "Foul on the arm," Coach DeCamp said. "Two shots."

The coach handed Ryan the ball on the foul line. Ryan glanced at the stands. Zeke, Eli, and Miles leaned forward on the edge of the bench. Benny's pen was poised above his notebook. Ryan wiped his suddenly damp palms against his shirt.

I wish I had practiced my foul shots instead of playing Ping-Pong, Ryan thought.

"Two shots," Coach DeCamp repeated.

Ryan bounced the ball three times, took a deep breath, and shot.

The ball bounced off the front of the rim and fell away.

I've got to make this one, Ryan thought as he dipped and shot again. This time the ball clanged off the back of the rim. Ryan jumped forward, straining for the rebound and hoping to make up for his two misses.

Phweeet! Coach DeCamp blew the whistle and pointed at Ryan. "Foul on Phillips, over the back," he said and then turned to the players in the stands. "Let's switch teams. Teams one and five on the floor. Let's hustle."

Ryan halfheartedly slapped hands with Zeke and Eli as his two buddies walked onto the floor. Miles tossed Ryan a towel as Ryan slumped onto the bench.

"Man, I played lousy," Ryan said, disgusted.

"You did okay," Miles assured him.

"Yeah, right," said Ryan. "No points, no rebounds, two missed foul shots, plus a stupid foul."

"At least the coach calls you by your name," Miles said.

"What?"

"The coach said your name when he called the last foul," Miles pointed out. "He's been watching you. He knows who you are." Miles sighed. "The coach has never called me by my name."

Ryan sat on the bench watching the scrimmage and thinking about what Miles had said. *Maybe the coach has been watching me,* Ryan thought, *but that doesn't mean I'll make the team.*

Staring out at the game, Ryan compared himself with the other Sligo Stallion hopefuls. *Frankie's not that great a ball handler. I play better defense than Ian does. Nicholas is kind of short to play forward.*

He secretly wished that all the players would mess up and miss their shots except Zeke, Eli, and Miles.

Ryan's thoughts were interrupted when Coach DeCamp called, "Okay, switch it up. Let's have teams two and five on the floor this time."

Ryan bounced off the bench, eager for another chance to show what he could do. Right away, Ryan got a pass at his favorite spot on the wing. He faked a pass to Drew Moyers, spun past the defender, and slipped in for a twisting layup.

Zeke jumped off the bench as the ball fell through the net.

"All right, Ryan!"

"Sweet move. Sweet move."

The next time down the court, Ryan took a pass a little farther out on the wing. Without hesitating, Ryan let fly a long jump shot past the leaping defender.

Swish.

Zeke was on his feet, his arms pushed high in the air in a wide V. "Three-pointer!" he shouted. "Three-pointer!"

Ryan could not help smiling as he ran by the bench where Zeke was shouting. Coach DeCamp took the whistle out of his mouth. "Nice shot, Phillips," the coach said.

THIRTEEN

Rrrrring, rrrring.

"I got it," Ryan's little sister Natalie said as she ran to the phone.

Ryan sat in the living room with his mother. She was reading the front page of the Sunday paper and Ryan was studying the sports section.

"It's for you, Ryan."

"Who is it?" he asked as he put down the paper.

"Zeke," she said, holding the phone out for Ryan and mouthing the word, "again!"

"Don't stay on too long, Ry," his mother called. "You still have homework to do."

"Not much," he replied, and took the phone.

"Hi. What's up, Zeke?" Ryan said.

"I was just talking to Nathan Harmata," Zeke said, the words tumbling out in excitement. "And he said the coach has already posted the list of kids who made the team. It's on the wall outside the gym."

"How does he know?"

"He rode over to the school and looked in the back door by the gym."

"Could he see any names on the list?" Ryan asked, suddenly as excited as Zeke.

"No, the door is too far from the list. But Eli and I are going down first thing tomorrow to check it out when school opens."

"What about Miles?" Ryan asked. "Is he going too?"

"No," Zeke said. "He said he'd go by later. You want us to swing by and get you?"

Ryan felt his stomach tighten. "Yeah," he said at first. But then suddenly he changed his mind. It would be too embarrassing to be with Zeke and Eli if he wasn't on the list. "No, I'll...I'll...you know, I'll just go by myself."

"Okay, have it your way," Zeke said.

Ryan, sensing there wasn't much more to say, said, "Good luck."

"Don't worry," Zeke said confidently. "We'll make it."

"I hope so," Ryan said. "See you tomorrow."

Ryan walked back to the living room, thinking about the single sheet of paper on the wall outside the gym. His mother was reading to his sister Natalie as the two cuddled together with the comics.

"Can I go downstairs for a couple of minutes before I do my homework?" Ryan asked.

"Okay," his mother said.

Ryan walked through the kitchen. Max was pouring himself some coffee. "Hey, Ry, I'll play you in a game of Ping-Pong," he said.

Ryan looked up. "Sure," he said.

"I'll be down as soon as I finish this," Max said, holding up his cup of coffee.

Ryan went downstairs and turned on the lights. The room was empty and quiet. The Ping-Pong paddles lay on the table where the boys had left them.

Ryan wandered over to the chair next to the Ping-Pong table and picked up Zeke's list. He sat on the edge of the chair and placed the paper on the Ping-Pong table. He studied the names and the check marks, hoping that if he stared at the paper and concentrated long enough, Zeke's predicted lineup for the school team would come true.

"You ready for our game?" Max said as he entered the room. He grabbed a paddle from the table.

"Oh. Yeah...ah...sure...." Ryan said.

"Who's the champ among your friends?"

"You're looking at him," Ryan said proudly. "Actually, Zeke says he is."

Max nodded and then pointed at the paper with his paddle. "What's that?"

"Just a list of some kids trying out for the basketball team," Ryan said. "Zeke was trying to figure out who would make it."

"Did he figure you'd make it?"

"Yeah." Ryan nodded as he picked up his paddle. "But I wish I could be as sure as Zeke."

"Well, you'll find out tomorrow."

"Max," Ryan asked, "did *you* ever get cut from a team?"

"Sure," Max replied with a laugh. He thought for a moment. "I remember when I was in the ninth grade I tried out for my ninth-grade basketball team and didn't make it," he said as he bounced the ball up and down on his paddle. He caught the ball and continued. "Of course, I was small for my age. I hadn't hit my growth spurt and it seemed like everybody else had. So I didn't expect to make the basketball team." He looked at the paddle, shook his head and said, "But I really thought I was going to make the *baseball* team."

"What happened?" Ryan asked.

"Well, we had a week of tryouts and I did pretty well. I hit the ball well. I was a good fielder, not great, but good enough. I even got the school physical that they gave to all the kids who play on the school teams. All the kids, including me, were sure that I was going to be on the team. But when the coach posted the team roster, my name wasn't there." His voice trailed off, sounding far away. Then he chuckled to himself. "I even remember the kid who made the team instead of me."

"Who?"

"Peter Nagle. He was a big kid. We used to call him 'Pugsley.'"

"Why didn't you make it?"

"I was pretty small and kind of slow," Max laughed again. "Not a very good combination for baseball."

"Did you ever play baseball after that?" Ryan asked.

"Yeah. I played in a Babe Ruth League, but never on a school team." Max spun his paddle in his hand. "Come on, I thought we were going to play a game."

"I really hope I make the team. I've got a pretty good shot at it," Ryan said, moving from the side of the table.

"I hope you make it, too, Ry," Max said. "But if you don't, that will be okay. You know—"

Ryan interrupted. "I know, Michael Jordan got cut from his varsity team."

"Really? I didn't know that," Max said. "I was going to tell you that Bill Russell didn't make his high school team on his first try."

"Bill Russell? Who's he, a friend of yours?"

"Not exactly," Max said with a wide grin. "Bill Russell played center for the Boston Celtics. He won eleven NBA championships in thirteen years."

"Wow! That's more than Michael Jordan."

"Yeah. I'll bet a lot of good players get cut sometime in their career. But that doesn't stop them. They keep playing the game," said Max. Then he pointed to the table. "Hey, enough already. We've got a game to play right here. Let's volley for serve."

Max bounced the ball across the table to Ryan.

"Good luck," Max said.

FOURTEEN

Thumpa, thumpa, thumpa, thumpa.
Ryan could hear his heart pounding harder with each step as he ran up the winding concrete walkway to the school. His mouth was dry, and the sour taste of his morning orange juice stuck in the back of his throat.

No kids were around. The bell for the first class was still a half hour away. Ryan looked around for Zeke and Eli but didn't see them. The side door leading to the gym was open. Inside, the doorway looked dark and forbidding, like the mouth of a cave.

Ryan was almost out of breath as he walked through the door. He hesitated for a moment to let his eyes adjust to the dim light. Down the short hallway, he saw the list. Two seventh graders were walking away from it, shaking their heads in disappointment. *No way those two made it,* Ryan thought.

Ryan could barely feel the hard linoleum

floor beneath his feet as he walked slowly down the empty hallway. His heart beat wildly. *Thumpa. Thumpa. Thumpa. Thumpa.*

Finally his eyes focused on the list. He studied the plain black names on the white paper taped firmly at the corners to the wall. Ryan's mind was a jumble of names and thoughts as he read down the list.

*The following individuals should report for boys' basketball practice tomorrow at 3:00 P.M. Antoine Daniels...Eddie Wilson...*I guess he passed math...*Eli Powell...*so the big guy made it!...*Frankie Reilly...Ian Will...Edward Zilkowski–*Zeke! All right, Zeke made it!...*Patrick Barrow... Nathan Harmata...Alex Kaess...Andrew Kaess....* I knew Coach would take some seventh graders...*Matthew Finn...Dustin Henry.*

Ryan looked at the names again. But the list did not change. His name was not there. Neither was Miles's or Drew's or so many others.

Ryan had not made the team.

A bit dazed, Ryan wandered down the hall, fighting back the urge to run home. He turned the corner of the corridor and saw Zeke and Eli standing beside their lockers. *I can't avoid them the rest of my life,* Ryan thought. "Hey guys," he said, trying to keep the disappointment out of his voice.

The two boys turned around. The smiles on their faces suddenly vanished.

"Hey, Ryan," Zeke said, trying to sound as if everything was fine.

"Hey, Ryan," Eli said. Both boys shuffled their feet and looked at the floor.

"Congratulations. I saw you made the team," Ryan piped up, breaking the awkward silence.

"There's no way the coach should have left you off the team," Zeke said a little too loudly. "You're better than half the guys who made it."

Eli nodded in agreement. "You should have made it, Ryan."

Ryan managed a weak smile. "I always said I wished you could pick the team, Zeke," he said. "Look, I've gotta go. I need to grab some stuff out of my locker before classes start." He started down the hall.

"Hey, Ryan," Zeke called. Ryan turned. "We're still friends, right?" Zeke asked.

"Sure." Ryan nodded. "We're just not team-mates."

FIFTEEN

The next afternoon, Ryan halfheartedly threw darts at the dartboard in the basement. Miles leaned forward on the edge of a chair and played a slow, bluesy tune on his sax. The basement seemed strangely empty without Eli and Zeke.

Ryan sank the final dart deep into the board. "You want to play Ping-Pong or something?" he asked Miles.

"Not really," Miles said. "Looks like you'll be the Ping-Pong champ for a while."

"What do you mean?" Ryan asked.

"With Zeke and Eli playing on the team after school, there's nobody to challenge you."

"What about you?"

"This is my game," Miles said as he held up his sax. "I'm going to concentrate on my sax. I think I'm going to try out for the Sligo jazz band."

"You'll make it," Ryan said confidently.

"I hope so," Miles said. "But I thought I might make the basketball team and that didn't happen."

Ryan flopped back into his chair. "Man, I sure wish I had made the basketball team," he groaned.

"Well, maybe you'll turn out to be like—"

"Like Michael Jordan?" Ryan finished the thought for Miles. "Yeah, right."

Miles glanced at his watch. "I've gotta get going," he said, putting his sax into its case. "I've got a music lesson in fifteen minutes. New teacher."

After Miles left, Ryan was all alone. He missed the way things used to be. He missed the usual noises. The *plick-plock* of the Ping-Pong ball. All of the guys' jokes and teasing. Ryan even missed Zeke claiming he was the champion at everything.

Ryan started feeling sorry for himself. It seemed like he had lost more than just a place on the team.

Finally, Ryan stood up and grabbed a basketball from the corner of the basement. *Well, if I'm going to be like Michael Jordan,* he thought, *I'd better start practicing.*

He walked upstairs and called out, "I'm

going down to the park to shoot some baskets."

"Okay," his mom said. "Be back by five o'clock. It starts getting dark early."

As Ryan dribbled to the park, pounding the ball against the pavement, he kept thinking about the list and the team. *Zeke was right,* he thought, *I'm better than half the kids on that list. I should have made the team.*

It was an unusually mild day for mid-December and a bunch of younger kids were hooping it up at the park on one of the basketball courts. Ryan found an empty court and started working on his game. He dribbled, shot, and rebounded the ball with more determination than ever. He dribbled so hard, it was as if he were pounding out his anger and disappointment. He was so focused on practicing that he didn't see the kid riding a bike nearby.

"Hey, Ryan."

Ryan stopped and looked around. Drew Moyers stood at the edge of the court, straddling his bike. "Mind if I play too?" Drew asked.

"I guess not. Come on," Ryan said. Drew put down his bike and Ryan took a shot and tossed him the ball.

"Mind if I play too?" Drew asked.

Drew dribbled and put up a jumper that bounced off the rim and fell away.

Drew smiled. "Maybe that's why I'm down here with you instead of in the gym practicing with the team."

Ryan picked up the ball and tossed it back. "I thought for sure you'd make the team," Ryan said. "You made it last year."

"I took too many dumb shots during try-outs," Drew said. "And Coach said I've got to work on other parts of my game too, like passing to other players."

Ryan laughed. "Yeah, I think the coach might have a point."

Drew laughed too, but not as hard as Ryan. Then Ryan put up a jumper. *Swish.*

"You know," Drew said, chasing the ball, "I was sure you were going to make it."

"I guess I didn't shoot well enough, either," Ryan said. He was quiet for a moment, thinking back on tryouts. "So what are you going to do about playing hoop this winter?"

Drew spun to his left and canned a fifteen-foot jumper. "I'm signed up for a recreation league team," he said. "What about you?"

Ryan swished another jumper. "I'll probably play a lot of Ping-Pong," he joked.

"You any good?" Drew asked.

"Pretty good."

"I've played some Ping-Pong. Maybe I can give you a game sometime."

"Sure, anytime," Ryan said. "I'm glad to find some competition. I have a table in my basement."

Ryan's long jump shot rattled around the rim and fell through the net.

"Nice shot," Drew said. "You know that rec league team I play on—the level of play is pretty good. We could use a guy like you. I could tell the coach about you, if you want to play."

"Sure," Ryan said eagerly.

Ryan and Drew kept playing as the winter darkness descended and seemed to steal the mild air away. They paid no attention to the growing cold and moved around the court, shooting, rebounding, and passing. The two boys didn't say much.

Finally Ryan grabbed a rebound and held on to the ball. "You know, I thought not making the team was the worst thing that could happen," he said, looking at Drew.

"Yeah, I felt awful when I didn't see my name on the list," Drew agreed. He held out his hands for the ball as Ryan flipped it to him and kept talking.

"We can still play ball for the rec teams and work on a few things, I guess," Ryan said. "And I can help you with your passing," he added kiddingly. "But really, if we keep up our skills we've got a good shot at making the team next year." Ryan broke for the basket but Drew dipped and sent a jumper spinning to the hoop.

"Yeah, you're right," Drew said, grabbing the ball that bounced high off the rim. "I guess I should have passed the ball to you just then," Drew said with a laugh. This time, Drew bounced a quick pass that Ryan caught in midstride and laid in the basket.

Ryan and Drew smiled at each other and slapped a lazy high five. "You know, we're not the only guys who have been disappointed about being cut," Drew said. "Did you know Michael Jordan got cut from his high school varsity team?"

Ryan almost laughed. He held the ball, thinking back to all the hours he and Zeke, Eli, and Miles had spent in Ryan's basement talking about Michael Jordan and dreaming about being teammates.

"Yeah, I heard something about that," Ryan said. Then he took one last shot.

Swish.

The Real Story

Michael Jordan of the Chicago Bulls is without a doubt one of the greatest basketball players of all time.

Michael has played on many championship teams—at the University of North Carolina, in the National Basketball Association (NBA), and in the Olympics. He is a ten-time NBA All-Star and a ten time NBA scoring champ. And Michael is not only a big star in America; he has fans all over the world.

But he wasn't born big and famous. As a kid in Wilmington, North Carolina, Michael Jordan was just one of the crowd. He wasn't the best basketball player in the neighborhood, or even the best basketball player in his family. His older brother Larry always beat him in one-on-one games. Michael learned a lot from him.

Basketball was just one of the sports Michael played as a kid. He was a pitcher on

Michael Jordan flies high over Hoggard High School defenders for the Laney High School Buccaneers in 1980.

his school's baseball team and a quarterback on the football team.

But in high school, Michael really started to get serious about basketball. By the time he was a sophomore, he had grown to 5'10" tall and played at point guard. Though he thought he was good enough for the school's varsity basketball team, he didn't make the final cut, and he spent the whole season playing with the junior varsity. His disappointment at not making varsity made him more determined to make it next time. The following summer he played basketball every chance he got. He worked hard on improving his skills. (He also grew five inches!)

When he started his junior year, Michael was bigger and better, and he had no trouble making the varsity team. But he didn't slow down after he made the team. He kept working hard. He went to his varsity practices, but he also kept going to junior varsity practices so he could get extra workout time. And by his senior year, Michael was an outstanding ball player.

Michael Jordan is not the only basketball star who struggled at the beginning. Boston Celtic center Bill Russell did, too. He is retired now, but when Bill Russell played, he was basketball's greatest winner. In college, he played on teams that won two championships, and in the pros, his teams won eleven NBA championships. Russell also played basketball in the Olympics, where his team won the gold medal.

Russell grew up in Oakland, California. As a kid, he was tall and clumsy. "I could run and jump, all right, but if there was a basketball within twenty feet of me, I went to pieces," he once said.

When he was a sophomore in high school, he tried out for the junior varsity basketball team. (He knew he didn't have a chance of making the varsity.) Sixteen kids tried out for fifteen spots. The team's kind coach, George Powles, did not have the heart to cut anyone.

Bill Russell prepares to sink a shot for the University of San Francisco Dons in the mid-1950s.

So Bill and a teammate had to share the fifteenth jersey. Though today Bill Russell is in the Basketball Hall of Fame, during his sophomore year in high school, he only played in half of the junior varsity games—he sat in street clothes behind the team's bench during the other games!

Like Michael Jordan, young Bill Russell kept practicing and kept growing. After his senior year in high school, he earned a basketball scholarship to the University of San Francisco and was on his way to becoming a basketball star.

Michael Jordan and Bill Russell got better because they didn't give up. They both kept playing and worked hard. And they learned that even if a player doesn't make the final cut one year, with hard work and dedication, that player may very well make the team next time.

Acknowledgments

Much of the information about Michael Jordan found in The Real Story chapter is from: *Hang Time: Days and Dreams with Michael Jordan* by Bob Greene, *Michael Jordan: Beyond Air* by Philip Brooks, *Sports Great: Michael Jordan* by Nathan Aaseng, *Michael Jordan: Basketball Skywalker* by Thomas R. Raber, and *Michael Jordan: A Biography* by Bill Gutman. The information about Bill Russell is from *Second Wind: The Memoirs of an Opinionated Man* by Bill Russell and Taylor Branch.

About the Author

One of the biggest disappointments of Fred Bowen's life was that he did not make his high school varsity basketball team in Marblehead, Massachusetts. But he did not stop playing. Mr. Bowen played pickup basketball and in recreational leagues for twenty-five years. He played on one team, the Court Jesters, for eighteen straight seasons.

Now Mr. Bowen coaches a kids' basketball team. In fact, he has been coaching the same kids for the past nine years—since they were in the first grade.

Mr. Bowen, author of *T.J.'s Secret Pitch, The Golden Glove, The Kid Coach, Playoff Dreams, Full Court Fever,* and *Off the Rim,* lives in Silver Spring, Maryland, with his wife and two children.

HEY, SPORTS FANS!
Have We Got Spectacular News For You!
Announcing...
The AllStar SportStory Series

Fan Club!

A fun way to learn more about these action-packed sports books that mix stories about regular kids playing ball with real sports history. We'll also tell you more about the author Fred Bowen (who's the biggest sports fan!) and his plans for upcoming books in the series.

When you join the club, we'll send you some really cool stuff...

★ An AllStar SportStory Series
Fan Club newsletter filled with great
sports facts, quizzes, stories, and everything
there is to know about these sports books

★ A book sticker autographed
by author Fred Bowen

★ An AllStar SportStory series ball card
(a perfect bookmark!)

★ A fan club membership card

Here's how you join...

1. Put your name, address, and a first-class stamp on a legal-sized envelope.

2. Ask your parents for a money order or check for $1.00 made payable to Peachtree Publishers (for shipping and handling). *Do not send cash in the mail.*

3. Tear out the form below and fill it out.

4. Put everything in an envelope and send it to:

The AllStar SportStory Series Fan Club
Peachtree Publishers
494 Armour Circle NE
Atlanta, GA 30324

(And, if you want, you can also send a letter to author Fred Bowen!)

- - - - - - - - - - - - - - - -

Your Name _____ Age_____

Your Address _____

City _____ State _____ Zip _____

Your School _____

Your Favorite AllStar SportStory Book _____

(Please allow 4–6 weeks for delivery)

Book Eight in the
AllStar SportStory Series—

ON THE LINE

Marcus is tall, his playing is terrific. He's the man all over the basketball court—except the foul line. Try as he might, Marcus just cannot get his foul shots to go in. Will Marcus be able to make the shots for his team when the game is on the line?

Look for Fred Bowen's
ON THE LINE
coming Fall 1999!